D0463180

By DAVID CORWIN

Illustrated by
HAWLEY PRATT and HARRY GARO

gb GOLDEN PRESS • NEW YORK

Second Printing, 1971

© Copyright 1962 by P.A.T.-Ward Productions, Inc.
All rights reserved.
Produced in U.S.A. by Western Publishing Company, Inc.

GOLDEN, A LITTLE GOLDEN BOOK, and GOLDEN PRESS®
are trademarks of Western Publishing Company, Inc.

Once there was a moose. He had big funny feet. He had a great big funny nose. And his name was Bullwinkle J. Moose.

He liked cup cakes and mooseberry juice. He had them three times a day—for breakfast, lunch, and dinner. And all day long, Bullwinkle dreamed that he was a brave firemoose.

In his daydream he climbed up to a burning roof. Smoke and cinders swirled all around him.

"Never fear," said Bullwinkle to a little old lady in his dream. "You are in my arms. Together we will jump safely to the safety net."

So, in his daydream, Bullwinkle jumped . . .

Babbump, he fell off his chair.

His friends, Rocky and Peabody, came rushing in.

"Ohhhh," groaned Bullwinkle. "What's the use? I'll never be a firemoose."

"I know what *I* would do if I were you," said Peabody, who was a very clever dog.

"What?" groaned Bullwinkle.

"I'd take a train and travel to the city," Peabody said. "And I'd go from firehouse to firehouse, until I'd get a job."

What a great idea!

Bullwinkle put his head up. His great big ears flapped back and forth. He gave a long happy honk.

"HONNNNNNNNKKKK!"

Rocky and Peabody held their ears.

The moose's honk was louder than a thunderclap. It could be heard miles away.

"Bully!" cried Bullwinkle. "I'm going to the city."

Off he pounded to the railroad station.

"*All aboooard!*" the conductor called. "*And no sticking antlers out of windows!*"

With a *click* and a *clack* and a *clickety-clack,* the train began to move.

Bullwinkle was on his way!

The *clicking* song the train made soon put the moose to sleep. And while he slept, he had a dream.

In the dream, Bullwinkle was putting out a fire with a firehose. Water was gushing from the hose in a steady stream, when suddenly—

Splash, he was drenched with water.

"Excuse me," said a little boy. "I spilled some water from this paper cup."

"No harm done," yawned Bullwinkle.

Just then, with a bump and a thump, the train stopped.

The conductor said in a worried voice:

"There's a herd of cows on the track. And our whistle isn't working. Without a whistle, we can't make the cattle move."

Everybody wondered what could be done.

"Stop worrying," said Bullwinkle. "My *honk* is louder than a thunderclap. It can be heard miles and miles away."

So Bullwinkle went up front. And he honked.

"HONNNNNKKKK...!"

The cows had never heard such a honk before. They bawled with fright, and ran away. And the train could go again.

At last the train came to the city, and Bullwinkle got off.

The conductor called after him:

"Thanks, Bullwinkle. We never would have reached the city, if not for you."

Whooooo. . . .

A siren wailed just then.

It was a gleaming red fire engine, returning from a fire.

Whooooo. . . .

With its siren wailing, the fire engine whizzed swiftly through the crowded city streets.

"Wait for me!" cried Bullwinkle as he pounded after it.

The fire engine reached the firehouse. And so did Bullwinkle, gasping for breath.

"Sir," he panted to the chief. "I'd like a job."

First the chief stared. Next he scratched his head. Then he began to snicker. And then he laughed with all his might.

"Don't be a silly goose," laughed the chief. "Who ever heard of a firemoose?"

Bullwinkle went from firehouse to firehouse. But all the chiefs just laughed at him. Not one would give him a job.

Poor Bullwinkle. He flopped down in front of the last firehouse, and he gave a heavy sigh.

"It's no use," he groaned. "I'll never be a fire-moose."

Ding, ding, ding. . . .

The alarm inside the firehouse began to ring.

Bullwinkle sadly watched the firemen slide down the poles.

He watched sadly as they jumped on the side of their fire engine.

Sadly he waited for the siren to go *Whooooo.*

But he never heard it. . . .

The chief said in a worried voice:

"The siren is broken. We can't speed through crowded streets without a siren. Nobody will hear us coming. And they won't get out of the way."

All the firemen wondered what could be done.

"Stop worrying," said Bullwinkle. "And never fear—Bullwinkle is here."

Bullwinkle sat up front.

He honked. And he honked. And he honked.

"HONNNNKKK . . .!"

Nobody in all the city had ever heard such a honk before. Holding their ears, they ran into their houses.

The fire engine whizzed swiftly through the empty streets. And it reached the fire just in time.

The chief shook hands with Bullwinkle.

"Thanks," he said. "We never would have been in time to put the fire out, if not for you."

"Here, Bullwinkle—take this helmet for your very own. For now you have a job."

What a job that was!
Smoke and cinders...

Up on burning roofs...

Steady streams
of gushing water...

But Bullwinkle saved seventy-seven little old ladies by jumping with them safely down to safety nets.

And he won a medal.

Now Bullwinkle is back home again.

He still likes cup cakes and mooseberry juice. And he has them for breakfast, lunch and dinner.

But he no longer dreams all day long.

With his helmet and his medal—Bullwinkle *knows* he is a brave firemoose!